Baby Blossom Makes a Wish

Based on the Original Flower Fairies™ Books
by Cicely Mary Barker

Frederick Warne

Every little fairy has to go to school before they can become a true Flower Fairy. Guelder Rose makes sure her sister Baby Blossom is in class bright and early to learn about plants, friendly magic and the secret Fairy Code.

But instead of listening to her kind fairy teachers, Baby Blossom's head is up in the clouds.

That evening she writes
in her diary…

Dear Diary,
My sister says
I must try harder with
my lessons, but I long to be
up in the trees with the
older fairies. All day
I dream of playing in
the branches and chasing
the butterflies!

Tomorrow I must learn how to make fairy wishes. I so want to wish, but how will I ever manage it if I can't sit still? I must try my very best and make my sister proud!

Jack-go-to-Bed-at-Noon arrives at
daybreak to teach the young fairies
how to wish. Baby Blossom and
her friends watch
carefully.

"I catch the first breeze of the morning," he tells them, puffing up his cheeks and blowing hard. "The wind carries the wishes far and wide, spreading my magic like fairydust."

Then Christmas Tree fairy shows
them how she weaves her wonderful
spells. "I close my eyes, let my
wings sparkle and tap my wand
twice," she says. "You each have
to discover your own special
way of wishing."

But while the other little fairies listen
closely, Baby Blossom has fluttered away.

By the time she has finished daydreaming, the class is busy practising wishes down in the meadow. She hurries to catch them up, and then she gets started. She has lots of things to wish for.

Baby Blossom closes her eyes and taps the twig twice, but nothing happens!

The poor fairy can't understand what has gone wrong.

Later Guelder Rose and the older
fairies stay up whispering in
the starlight. "Maybe your little
sister needs some friendly fairy
help," suggests Nightshade.
"I heard Baby Blossom crying
because she's bottom of
the wishing class."

"Let me sprinkle a special dream spell onto her pillow," says Poppy.

Here is Poppy's spell:

Before you can make fairy magic, you must discover your own way of wishing. Ask the Wishing Flower to help you. Sweet dreams, Baby Blossom!

Baby Blossom seeks out the beautiful white
Wishing Flower as soon as she wakes up.

"You're an enchanting little Tree Fairy
who loves to skip and float from leaf to leaf,"
sings the Flower. "Remember this and all
your wishes will come true."

In class, the fairies are learning to fly.
Baby Blossom looks up at the treetops
and wishes as hard as she can.
Suddenly she floats up in the air, using
her white blossom branch as a
delicate parachute.

"I'm a true fairy at last!"
she gasps. "Guelder Rose
will be so proud."

FREDERICK WARNE

Published by the Penguin Group
Penguin Books Ltd, 80 Strand, London WC2R 0RL, England
New York, Australia, Canada, India, New Zealand, South Africa

This edition first published by Frederick Warne 2004
1 3 5 7 9 10 8 6 4 2

ISBN 0 7232 4972 5

Printed in China